A Crime for Two

N.V Hill

Published by TaiLorMade Books

CHAPTER ONE

"I'm glad you finally decided to come over," he said.

"Yeah, well, when you work on a cop's schedule it's almost impossible to have a personal life."

"Are you sure you won't lose your badge for this? I mean... I'm pretty sure your buddies down at the precinct aren't too fond of me."

"Why are you acting like you care?"

"Well, I don't give a dam really. I just don't want that heat on my back. If we're going to be hanging out together, I feel there should be some boundaries."

"Such as?"

"For one, I don't feel comfortable discussing anyone I know that you guys may be looking for. Number two, I think we should keep things very low profile, you know?"

What a prick, she thought. *Parading you around anyone would be the last thing I'd ever do.*

"Trust me, you would be the last person that I would try to interrogate. I am a professional. I keep my personal life very discrete," she seductively stated, braising her hand across his manhood.

"Girl, you are a world wonder," he said, rising to the occasion.

"You have no idea."

An hour or so later it was finally over, and I couldn't be more elated. He snored beside me, the god-awful sounds vibrating his chest and erupting from his parted lips. His lips were turning black from cigarette smoke and marijuana, and they were full as though stacked with pus. I knew I was exaggerating about the fullness of his lips, but at least that gave an idea of just how much I found him repugnant.

Here he was, sound asleep beside me, unaware that his life was only a few breaths away from being extinguished. He wouldn't even get the chance to grant any final wishes. He would fade on to nothingness and not a soul would notice—unless of course they were people, who just like me, wanted him dead.

The bed was drenched with both our sweats—most of which our bodies had soaked up. We had spent the night engaging in a very steamy sex that had left him breathless. Being the insolent scum that he was, it hadn't taken long for him to fall asleep. For the first few moments after he'd given into sleep, I'd pretended to rest along with him. But I'd only done that to make sure he was knocked out cold.

He breathed, calm and lightly, unaware of an inescapable death looming in the air. Death was a woman, nude and fair-skinned, her legs still trembling from how intense the sex she'd just had was. She had a name—Crystal Jameson. And she was me—a twenty-nine-year-old bi-racial woman who had spent twenty years of her life fueling her flaming heart.

It didn't matter if the fire of my rage completely consumed me to the core. There was a gaping hole where love and sensitivity once resided. The only thing that mattered to me was finishing off what I had started, and there was only one way to. There was no turning back.

With my eyes fixated on him as he lay asleep, I shifted toward the edge of the bed. My moves were slow and tentative, and I was careful not to make a sound. Rousing him would only make this difficult in a way I hadn't planned for. This had to go smooth and easy, just like the others before it had. To be fair, I was even doing him a favor. He deserved no less than a slow, tortuous death. But now he'd die peacefully in his sleep, after having the sex of his life. Could there ever be a greater expression of humanity?

The mattress rustled underneath me, acknowledging my change in position. But its sound was only a soft whisper, audible to my ears alone. Even if it were louder, the slumbering man was far too spent to pick up any sound that wasn't related to the wet dream he was currently having.

Finally, at the edge of the bed, I flung my legs over it and rose to my feet. I crept across the room, my thighs bumping each other and bringing my attention to the slime—a disgusting mix of his sperm and my vaginal fluids—between them. I growled inwardly, hating the filth between my legs. If things were different, cleaning up the mess would be my next move. But I couldn't afford to do that at the moment. The sloshing sound from the bathroom would definitely awaken him, which was what I didn't want.

I moved over to the dressing table where my bag sat. He'd placed it there himself, unaware of what hid beneath the zipper. I slowly undid the zipper, my hand reaching deep inside the warmth of the bag. I fished around, only stopping once I gripped the cold metal of my SIG Sauer P220. I slowly pulled it out, narrowly escaping my personal effects that could bump into it and make a sound loud enough to rouse him. Fetching my silencer from the bag, I fastened it to the barrel and sauntered toward the side of the bed where he lay.

He slept on, unmoved. His chest rose and fell with each shallow breath he took. His thick skin lay concealed by a heavy carpet of hair on his chest. Patches of hair extended down his torso to his groin. They were strong and curly in the most disgusting way. It was a hell of a surprise that the sharp strands of hair hadn't bruised my skin. They had been scrubbing against me all through the duration of our intercourse. Bile rose to my throat—the memory of the past hour with this man did that to me.

My trigger finger grazed the trigger, eager to pull it already. I raised the gun in the air, with its barrel aimed at his chest, right where I knew his beating heart would be. My grip on the pistol tightened, flaunting my resolute resolve.

His eyes popped open, staring straight into mine. The look in his eyes was hard and cold, knocking me out of breath. For a moment, I was still as a statue, staring back at him. His gaze switched from my face to the gun barrel, and it was apparent he was thinking up an escape plan. Proving me right, he suddenly leapt off the bed, lunging at me.

"Crystal. Wait. You don't have to do this."

There was no time for conversation. Begging wasn't going to change his destiny. His fate was sealed the moment he had led me into his bedroom.

"Bitch!" he cursed.

That was the last word he would ever say.

I squeezed the trigger, taking a clean shot at him. One shot in his chest was all it took to end him, but for a good measure, I fired three consecutive shots to reassure he was dead. He slumped down like a log of wood, his body crashing into the bed, with his legs dangling off the sides.

Time to leave. I tore my eyes away from him and headed to the side of the bed where my clothes lay strewed the floor. He'd ripped them off me in desperation to see what lied beneath. *Fucking pervert. They never learn.* They were always so dumb they never saw *it* coming.

After I'd wrapped up my body in my clothes, I slipped my feet into my wedge shoes and grabbed my bag. I glanced around, making sure I wasn't leaving anything behind. I headed for the door, and as I took a final glance at the man's dead body, a crooked smile tugged at my lips. The man was Gregory Martinez, a thirty-two-year-old black Hispanic with several cases of carjacking, assault, and burglary under his name. And I, I was a police officer—I hunted bad guys for a living.

But was this why I had killed him and the ones before him?

No, I had my own reasons and they were personal.

Perhaps too personal.

CHAPTER TWO

I went home, cleaned my gun, and placed it back in the holster. I wasn't worried about being investigated because I knew they would never suspect me. I always wore a disguise and made sure I only went out at night when visiting my kill. Gloves and scarves were a must and I always wore a fashionable wig. It was fitted so perfect that you could never tell it wasn't my hair. It was one of the advantages of being bi-racial. I could always switch up my look.

I prepared myself as I rehearsed how I was going to survey the crime scene. I knew it was only a matter of time before my fellow colleagues would contact me to help with the investigation. Like all the other murders, I would present my false assumptions to them, create a false profile, and lead the case to a dead end.

My basement was more or less like an office at the station where I worked. Covering up the wall on one side of the room was a medium-sized evidence board, with newspaper cuttings of deaths, sex crimes, and a host of other crimes—petty and serious ones alike.

Police officer murdered by unidentified gunmen.

Following the headline on a 1998 newspaper was the picture of the police officer who'd been killed twenty years ago in Nashville, Indiana. I trailed my fingers across the man's picture, shooting him a pained look. My fingers were starting to tremble, and my heart constricting as I tried hard not to break down. Struggling to keep my trembling fingers up, I traced the man's name with my index finger.

Oliver Jameson. That man was my father. I'd been only nine years old at that time—too fantasied to understand he was never coming back. Thus, each new morning I'd wake up to the thought that perhaps that was the day he would return to me. But with each passing year I slowly realized he was never coming back. This left me with only one wish: the bad guys had to pay.

I desperately wanted his murderers to be brought to justice, even if it meant taking the law into my own hands. But I was only a child, powerless to do anything but accept the fact that the police had failed to bring my father—their colleague—the justice he deserved.

I'd thought it was impossible to move on after the tragedy that had rocked my life like an earth-shattering quake. But Alyssa stood by me through it all, teaching me to live again, and to actually smile again. We'd been best friends since we were in our diapers. She opened my heart to the hope of a brighter future shining through the darkness of my past and present.

But that was until a second tragedy struck.

I glanced down at a newspaper beside my father's, and my misty eyes devoured the headline.

Girl, 18, raped to death on her graduation night.

I remembered that night like it was yesterday. It was one of the happiest moments of my life and Alyssa and I were going to celebrate. We had gotten our bellies pierced and bought matching belly rings. Later that night, we decided that we would meet at a new club that had just had their grand opening. I suggested that Alyssa crash with me since the club was closer to my home, but she decided to get a hotel room, so she could meet up with her boyfriend Bobby after we left the club.

Bobby was a little too old for her in my opinion and he only visited her every other weekend. I assumed he was married or something, but he had told Alyssa he had a job that required him to travel often. I remembered wanting to say something. I wanted to tell her she deserved better, but I didn't. I didn't want to seem like that salty friend that was mad because I didn't have a man.

The next day, I received that dreadful phone call from Alyssa's mother. I didn't want to believe it. I couldn't believe it. My first instinct was to kill her boyfriend. I was sure it was him. But her scum-bag boyfriend was in another city with his wife, which was why Alyssa decided to go back to the club and hangout some more. Her mother had told me that this douche bag confessed everything to Alyssa on her graduation night, which is why she called her mother crying. *Why didn't she call me?* I remembered asking myself. *Why?*

I never had a chance to say goodbye, and just like in my father's case, the culprits were never found. I'd lost my best friend in the blink of an eye, and her murder soon became forgotten. Everyone, it seemed, forgot her as new mornings rolled in. Only her family still felt the sting of an eleven-year-old injury. The others had all forgotten, and the police had as well, just as they'd all forgotten my father.

But I would never forget. The pain had eaten so deep into my heart, poisoning it with a dark venom I didn't try to fend off. I wanted it to consume me, to make my heart the darkest it could be.

Losing my father and my best friend opened my eyes to the path I needed to take. After Alyssa's death, I'd known right away that the Crystal everyone knew would die, making way for a vengeful spirit to live in her stead.

And I'd been right to think that. Crystal Jameson was long gone. I was no longer my father's little daughter, but a cold-hearted officer with a twisted mind. Ever since dad's murder I'd wanted to be a police officer, to bring criminals to justice in my own twisted way. Hence, I'd done everything humanly possible to pursue my dreams of being an officer.

Back then in high school, I'd been known as 'the problem solver'. I'd spent my free-time solving cases of locker break-ins and graffiti on bathroom walls. Some wanna-be 'problem solvers' had risen after me, but they'd all paled in comparison to me, and it made me hopeful that when I finally became a police officer, things would be no different. I would be the best officer in the small town of Nashville.

Looking away from the newspaper article of my best friend, I let my eyes hover over the surrounding newspapers of crimes that had happened in Nashville in the past two decades. Each newspaper cutting held the image of the criminal associated with each offense, and four of them had been crossed out with a marker. Transferring the marker in my left hand to my right, I crossed out Gregory's image, ignoring his cold eyes as they continued to stare at me as though they still had life in them.

On to the next one. Anthony Esteban. He was Hispanic and black, similar to Gregory, but much more attractive. His body resembled a statue. Every muscle was molded to perfection, even his jaw bones. It was obvious how he used his prison time.

His eyes held a piercing look that reached deep into my heart, igniting a fire. I was just as nervous as I'd been when I had my first kill six years ago—maybe even more nervous. Even though there was no reason to be anxious, the awful feeling was one I couldn't shake off. Perhaps this was because I'd never dealt with his kind.

"Hello," Crystal answered, startled by her buzzing phone.

"Hey detective, Jameson. Hope I didn't catch you at a bad time."

"Oh, no. I was actually following up on a lead for this new case. What's up?"

"I was giving you a call because the chief needs you down at the station immediately."

"Okay, is there something I need to be filled in on beforehand?"

"Well, pretty much the usual. A Hispanic man in his early thirties, late twenties found shot to death. Same MO. They're thinking it's a copycat killer or a serial murderer on hand."

"Tell the chief I'll be right down."

Just like clockwork I knew they would call. However, my attention went back to my next target. This thirty-eight-year-old man was different from the others I'd ever dealt with. He was the first of his kind in my timeline of vengeance. His crimes were mostly violent offenses including sexual battery. He had been charged with thirty-one counts of aggravated assaults—including twelve counts of sexual assaults with deadly weapons—over the past few years.

The thought that I was just about to lure an experienced sex-offender to bed chilled me to the bones. What if he subdued me instead of me subduing him? What if I became a victim in the end?

CHAPTER THREE

After moving on from the Martinez case, it was time for me to spring back into action. It only took about a week to down play his murder into a revenge crime. It was always feasible that a criminal of this nature had ex crime partners that felt jilted from deals gone wrong or had gained new enemies from the crimes they committed against other people.

I decided it was time to switch up the scenery and do something that I enjoyed. I hadn't spoken to my mother in a few days, so I figured I'd take her shopping with me. She said that she had a hair appointment but would love to go after she was finished. It wasn't like she had anything else to do. My mother decided not to date after the death of my father. And if she did, I never knew about it. Besides, her agreeing to go with me was the perfect solution to my minor dilemma. I would pick up my mom and drop her off at the stylist. Then, I could head to the Bloomington Mall about forty-five minutes out and take care of some personal business there. After that, I would go back to pick up my mom and go to one of the local shopping centers. It worked out even better than I expected.

After arriving at the mall, I surveyed the scene. As a cop, it's always a habit to be aware of my surroundings. I went in the mall, grabbed a few sale items, and spotted exactly what I was looking for. I headed to the car in what seemed like perfect timing.

"Damn it. This was just what I needed." I muttered, frozen in time.

I had just rammed my Cadillac CTS into the Ford Ranger beside mine. We'd both parked our vehicles outside the shopping mall. Somehow, I'd miscalculated the space between my vehicle and his'. I didn't want any mall security to get involved, so I hurried and put my car back in its regular position.

I could flee the scene at once; the owner of the Ranger was not in sight after all. He would be here any moment. But if I did flee, then he would never know that I hit him. How much damage had I caused his vehicle?

Stepping out of my car, I lit a cigarette as I walked over to inspect the damage. It wasn't particularly serious, but it was just enough to dent the exterior of the car. Perhaps if it was an older vehicle the damage would be forgivable. However, this truck was brand new. So new that it still had the drive-out tags.

"What the hell have you done to my vehicle?" a hoarse voice boomed from behind.

Although I'd been expecting him, his voice startled me anyway. It was deep and masculine, drenched with a threat that was anything but empty. He stormed toward me with two shopping bags in his hands, and I stared at him through the window of his Ranger.

"What the hell?" he asked again. He was closer this time, his footsteps shuffling toward me. "What have you done to my vehicle?"

Once within range, he placed his shopping bags on the ground and assessed the damage. He yanked me by the arm, almost knocking the cigarette out of my hand as he whirled me around to face him.

"Are you deaf, lady? What the hell have you done to my vehicle?" he yelled into my face.

With him so close to me, menacing and enraged, I couldn't help but give way to an involuntary shudder.

"It was an accident!" I said, my voice wobbling as he gripped my other arm and shook me violently.

"You shouldn't have done this," he said. His voice was noticeably calmer now, yet the threat lingered in its undertone.

"I'm sorry," I said.

"You think just a mere word is enough to undo the damage? This is a brand-new truck, lady," he yelled.

"I'll pay for damages. I will follow you to the nearest body shop, so we can get an estimate." I offered. It was a minor damage anyway. It wouldn't cost a lot.

"I don't trust you, lady. I can't believe this shit. Mi hermana is going to kill me."

"Look, I'll call my insurance company and we'll get this squared away right now."

"I'm not getting any pendejos involved in my shit."

"How did you get a new truck without insurance?"

"Fuck you!" He let go of me and stuck out his middle finger. Picking up his shopping bags with both hands, he said, "I'll let you go this time but the next time..."

Trailing off, he shook his head and started to pull away.

"I... I challenge you to a poker war," I shouted out after him.

He froze. I smoked inwardly. I had him right where I wanted him. Surely, he wouldn't say no to an offer as juicy as this.

It was the infamous Anthony Esteban. He was wanted for violent crimes, sex offenses, and everything else under the sun and now, I had finally tracked him down. If I were a fisherman, I would think my elation would be comparable to catching the biggest fish ever. I had been studying him for weeks now and gathered everything I could possibly find. I looked through his police file and got every residence that he had stayed at for the last five years. Although he had spent the majority of those years locked up, there were still a few known places he would go during his short breaks. The search wasn't as difficult as I had assumed it would be.

I found out he was living with his sister and two nephews. The truck that he drove wasn't in his name, but during my surveillance, I discovered he was the only one driving it. He kept a very low profile and he didn't go out much. I thought it was going to be impossible to catch him alone until I found out one of his routines. Every Wednesday he went to the Bloomington Mall to pick up a special package from one of the stores.

"Not interested." He yanked open the door to the driver's side of his Ranger and went to hop in the seat.

But then he halted, apparently reconsidering. He glanced back at me. My heart thumped as his eyes met mine. It looked as if his eyes started tracing the curves in my hips that were purposely accentuated in my leopard leggings and high-heels. I was blessed with D cups and a tiny frame. Sometimes I found myself to be irresistible.

"What happens if you lose?" he asked.

"If I lose, I'll foot the bills," I said.

"Senora, I have money. That's obviously not an issue."

"Well, what do you suggest?"

"Do I get to fuck you?" he asked.

My mouth went dry at his rawness. Is this the way he responded to all the women he encountered? I could only imagine what he would do if he got rejected. Perhaps with his handsomely devilish looks, he didn't get rejected often. On top of that, I hadn't expected a rapist to have even an ounce of modesty in him, or had I?

"I think I'd like that," I said. "As hard and rough as you want. I'll be yours for a whole night."

He may have been a heartless criminal, but he also was a typical guy. When it came time for a man to get his rocks off, nothing else mattered.

He grinned, his eyes flashing with the wildest blend of lust. "Well then, let's play poker."

CHAPTER FOUR

With each card played, piece after piece of clothing dropped to the floor. When it came to poker, I was queen. Defeat had never been a thing for me, so it was only natural that I was dazed to find myself on the losing end. Anthony was apparently a king of his own, gaining the highest hand every step of the way, while I lost a hand at almost every turn.

Anthony and I sat on a bed in a hotel room—we'd agreed to meet here for the poker war. I'd been so sure I'd win, but here I was, stripped of every piece of clothing and accessories except my G-string. The only articles of clothing he'd had to strip were his shirt and undershirt. His pants were still in place. It didn't take long before he won all the cards on the deck. I, on the other hand, had run out of cards. He looked up at me, his gaze lingering on my pantie.

"You lose," he said in a husky voice. His speech was laden with all the arousal that had been building up inside of him for half an hour now.

He hadn't made much conversation since the start of the game. He asked me a few questions about where I was from and my age. I guess everything else was irrelevant for the time being. Instead he'd chosen to communicate with a nod of his head, a wolf whistle or a wiggle of his brows whenever I stripped off an article of clothing.

"Take that off," he said, tilting his head toward my pantie.

I moved my hands to my pantie, trailing my fingers around the elastic band at the top of it. My vagina was gushing with so much wetness that I suddenly felt self-conscious. He would think of me as a slut once he got to see how wet I already was. But what did it matter? I would kill him right after he fucked me. So, I had nothing to worry about, or did I?

"Take off that damn underwear." His voice was a firm command.

I slowly slid the thin cotton down my ass. Anthony was not one with a lot of patience, I soon realized. His rapist instincts kicked in and he pounced on me, pinning me to the bed with his weight. His right hand scrambled between my thighs and grabbed my pantie. He tore it off me as though it were a sheet of paper. He heaved himself off me to rid himself of his bottoms. Once undressed, he tossed the clothes off to the other side of the room and lowered his muscular body to mine, crushing me underneath his weight. His chest was hard against my breasts, and my nipples strained hard against his skin.

He reached between his legs and gripped his manhood. He guided it to my openness, simultaneously nudging my legs apart with his strong thighs. The tip of his penis pressed hard against the entrance of my vagina, and then he tore his way in. His penis was probably the largest I'd ever had to take in, because I could hear him grunting while he rocked back and forth in a frantic effort to fully slide in. I slipped my hands down his torso, stopping only when I reached the firm globes of his butt cheeks. Groping them, I added pressure on them, urging him to go deeper. I was just as hungry for him as he was for me.

He reached behind his back to pry my hands off his skin, and then he gripped them at the wrists, pinning them to the bed. His penis strained harder against me. He grunted. I whimpered, flicking my wrists to free them, but he didn't give me a chance. Veins were starting to throb on his forehead. He clenched his teeth, a throaty grunt emerging from his mouth. With that, he invaded deep inside of me with one forceful thrust. I cried out from a sharp burst of pain. The man was large, too damn large. And I found that I appreciated a man even more when he had a penis large enough to bring me pain amidst pleasure.

He thrust in an out, starting to build a slow rhythm. And with each thrust, all my defenses seemed to break away. I could feel my walls loosening around him, fully accommodating him. While he lodged deep inside of me, I could feel him stretching to his limit. His thrusts were long and deep, hitting my core each time. It shoved me over the edge of my sanity, forcing me to breathe out in hoarse ragged bursts.

My cries of ecstasy were all over the place as I lost myself to the pleasure. It didn't matter that I would have to kill him before the end of the night. Right now, all I wanted was to lose myself to the pleasure as he tossed me into a whole new world. Slowly and slyly, I felt my vengeful spirit sail out of me, leaving in its wake a hormone-crazed beast. At this moment, I was just another woman. Nothing felt better than spending the night with a robust man who was good at his craft. Anthony Esteban was that man—my stud for the night.

The next day I felt pathetic as I lied in my own bed looking up at the ceiling feeling a bit of soreness between my legs. How could I allow a common criminal to redirect my objective? This wasn't like me. I trained myself to fuck and kill, not have second thoughts because of a rock-hard penis. But I admit the orgasm was magical. It was a feeling of euphoria that I hadn't experience.

A funny feeling ran through me. A feeling that I hadn't experienced and couldn't understand. I continued to ask myself. *Why was this so difficult? What happened to my relentless quest for vengeance?* Could one hard penis make me this soft? It didn't make sense for me to gain some sort of good conscious at this point. Hell, I was well on my way to intentionally killing almost half a dozen men; more than that if you count the ones killed in the line of duty.

My thoughts were as bipolar as a mental patient in a therapy session. There was a side of me that wondered if this man was the only man that would be able to give me that extent of gratification.

Who was I kidding? I knew that there was such thing as karma, but for me my actions were justified due to the injustice I had experienced. Regardless, I had to get my mind back focus on the subversion. I needed to find a way to get my edge back. I needed to do something that would suppress these inner thoughts and bring back that vengeful spirit that started this ordeal. I got up, got dressed, and went to visit my father's grave site.

I arrived at the cemetery feeling perplexed. Perhaps this wasn't a good idea after all. There were a few people in the distance hovering over deceased love ones and adjusting flowers place on the grave sites. I walked over the mushy rain-soaked grass and kneeled in front of my father's remembrance stone. The words engraved in it is what made me take the initiative to join the force.

Upstanding Officer, Dedicated Father

It all became too much. I hadn't visited here since Alyssa's death and coming today was a bad idea. I missed him so much. If only I could run up to him and wrap my arms around his neck. My tear ducts began to fill as a warm light stream flowed down my cheeks. It was almost as if I felt his presence. It felt like he was telling me that I had taken other kid's fathers away as he had been taken from me. This was not what I wanted. I needed to feel anger not remorse. I ran to the car and grabbed my phone. I scrolled through the pictures that Alyssa and I had taken that fatal night after our graduation. I always kept them in my phone. Not only to remember her, but to make sure I kept my promise to her. I promised that I would kill every crook that mimicked her murderer. I also had uploaded pictures that mom sent of dad and I on birthdays and

Christmas. The hatred had begun to build. I was ready. I called Anthony and set up another outing with him. Only this time, I was killing him for sure.

CHAPTER FIVE

"What are we doing here? This is supposed to be an address to a hotel," Crystal complained.

"Take it easy, Senorita. I told you I had something nice planned for you."

They had arrived at a cabin resort about twenty-five miles outside of town. Although Crystal was reluctant, she had to play along if she wanted to get the job done. He grabbed her hand as he opened the door into a candlelit dinner. A dozen white, red, and yellow roses were sitting in a mosaic vase on top of the table. The flowers were accompanied by champagne on ice and two crystal glasses half way full.

"I like my presentations to have a meaning. I brought crystal glasses to represent your exquisite beauty and the half-full glasses represent the optimism of our companionship despite our first encounter."

Crystal was beyond impressed. Perhaps the sex was as good to him as it was to her. Why else would he go out of his way to create such an ambience? He didn't know much about her. He said he didn't need money. What else would compel him to be so romantic in such a short period of time?

"I must admit this is very nice. Thank you."

"I'm sure a pretty girl such as yourself is use to this type of treatment, no?"

"Not really. I don't get to date much due to my work."

"What was it that you said you did?"

Almost choking on her champagne during the swallow, she didn't anticipate the question. She didn't mean to bring up work; it just slipped out without thought. "I uh… I work as a traffic operation specialist."

"Oh… sounds interesting."

"How about you? What do you do?"

"I have my private businesses going. I buy, remodel, and resale houses for a living. I dib and dabble in the auto world as well, but fixing houses is my passion."

"That sounds rewarding. Perhaps one day you could take me to one of the homes your working on and I could see the before and after process firsthand."

"Perhaps so. But you know what I would like to see."

"No, but I'm sure you're going to tell me."

"I would like to see those titties bouncing up and down while you ride this dick."

He was definitely rugged but for some reason it aroused me. I immediately unraveled my scarf and unbuttoned my long-sleeved shirt, just enough for my push-up bra to expose my emphasized breast. He tugged on my black skinny-jeans as I began to pull them down. His hunger for me had me even more excited. I quickly unbuckled his pants that were already unzipped and wrapped my hand around his solid stick. He grabbed my hips and forcefully sat me on top of him. I felt wild, untamed, and free in a sense.

Although there was a minor scuffle getting his penis to fully submerge inside, I wiggled my hips from side to side, so he could penetrate my walls. Once he was in, he grabbed my torso and threw me back and forth, coining the term of riding a hung horse. He stopped, snatched off my shirt, and roughly pulled up the bra, leaving minor scratches on my skin from both sides of my upper chest.

I moaned loudly as he continued to plunge his hardness in my constricted hole, creating a tingling sensation that escalated my orgasm. He gently bit down on my nipple. He knew he was taking me to ecstasy. He enjoyed being in control of my body. He was a criminal, so that wasn't a surprise.

"Uh…Uh…Uhhh!" I yelled as I climaxed on his penis that was now shaking sperm inside of me.

I sat up in bed, propping my back up on the backrest. My eyes were transfixed on Anthony as he lay sound asleep beside me in his unclothed state, with the comforter covering up his nudity. He was totally spent from our heated sex session that night, and so was I.

My handgun was right beside me, buried inside my handbag sitting on the nightstand; but although it was right beside me, it was out of reach. I just couldn't bring myself to pick it up and put a hole through his chest.

Damn it, there's no way around this. I had to kill him. It was a promise I'd made to my father and my best friend. I'd sworn to kill any criminal who ended up in bed with me. Why then was it so hard to kill him?

I decidedly left the question unanswered. I was unprepared to come to terms with the reason behind my indecision. It would be a lot more difficult if I accepted it, even to myself. When I'd been unable to kill him after our first night together, I'd comforted myself with the plan of killing him on our next night together. Little had I known that the poker night would be the first of many more passionate nights of intense love-making.

There was something about him. It wasn't just about how good in bed he was. There was something more—a trait that pulled me to him like a magnet, weakening my resolve to actualize my original plan. It was hard to believe I'd been with him a few weeks already, and thoughts of starting a family with him were already running through my mind.

But was that enough reason to let him live? Was that enough reason to go back on the promise I'd made to two people who mattered to me? Was a man like him deserving of a second chance, an opportunity to right his wrongs?

CHAPTER SIX

About two months or so had passed since Anthony and I had started seeing each other. Anthony decided to temporarily stay at a weekly pay hotel, so we could have somewhere homier to go for our sexual escapades. I knew he'd never take me to his sister's house because he didn't trust me. He had every right not to. Besides, I wasn't sure if I was even interested in meeting his family. I began to question everything.

I had figured keeping my occupation a secret would be proven to be difficult, but it turned out the opposite. Anthony wasn't the type of guy that made surprise calls or show up at my job unexpectedly. He was just as standoffish as I was.

Perhaps since I had told him I worked all type of hours on swing shifts, he had no problem waiting until I reached out to him. It didn't bother him that I didn't contact him much during the day. Sometimes I would go a few days without calling. It never mattered to him. He wasn't a man of many questions. Against my better judgement, I had decided to let him spend the night at my place.

I had not heard another report of Anthony sexually abusing anyone. Better yet, his remodeling business turned out to be legit. He seemed like a rehabilitated person. According to him, for the past few months he'd not been sexually involved with anyone else but me. As I watched him sleep beside me, I wasn't sure if I trusted him just yet, but I found myself believing his words.

Perhaps I was looking for something good to believe about him. The fact of the matter was, I had found out I was pregnant. It wasn't something I had planned, but I know that I didn't take the necessary precautions to prevent it either. *Was I even the motherly type?* How could I explain to my kid that his dad is a known sex offender with a criminal rap sheet as long as his Santa's list? The better half of me screamed abortion, but there was a tiny piece inside screaming this was my destiny. Although I had killed plenty of men, was I capable of destroying the creation growing inside of me?

I decided that I wasn't going to tell Anthony for obvious reasons. Although I had prolonged his execution date, I didn't permanently dismiss it. This sudden development only complicated the matter even more than it already was. My thoughts and feelings were a huge mold of atrocity.

Maybe this was it. Maybe my vengeance had ended after I killed Gregory. Perhaps it was time to rebuild my life, start a family and move on from the past. My father would want me to settle down, and Alyssa would want that too.

I was only a few months from clocking thirty. Years ago, when Alyssa was still alive, we'd both dreamt of finding our Mr. Rights when we were only in our early twenties. And at thirty, we figured we would already have kids.

I still couldn't get over how much things had changed. If Alyssa and my father were here, they would be unable to recognize the woman that I had become. Would they even understand that this was what I'd become for them? Prior to my father's death, I'd savored the hope of being a top-rated makeup artist when I grew older. Although as a child I admired the fact that my dad was a superhero, beauty was my thing. My mom would sit me down and show me how to apply concealer, foundation, and then blush in the basic makeup application process. She even allowed me to help her blend her eye shadows. But life, it seemed, decides our paths for us.

I looked down at Anthony again as he continued to sleep beside me. Was it remorse I felt for him? Where was remorse when my father was murdered in cold blood? Where was remorse when Alyssa was raped to death? And where was remorse when Anthony went about terrorizing people and raping innocent women as he stole their futures away from them? Where was remorse and all its pithiness?

The pistol in my bag called out to me. It would only take one shot; just a second and it would all be over. I reached for my handgun, my hand sinking into my bag to find it. Just as I grasped it, the bed groaned. Anthony was awake, shifting into a more comfortable position. I yanked my hand out of the bag. My face was pale as a ghost.

"Babe," he said, "Are you okay?"

I nodded. "Yeah."

He stared at me a little more intently. "You sure? You look pale, no?"

"I…uh…" I rubbed my left palm across my forehead. "I'm just having a little headache. That's all."

"Shit!" he sat upright in bed, touching my left hand. "How long have you been like this?"

"I woke up this way," I said.

"There's a seven-eleven store just around the corner." He scrambled to his feet and hastily clothed himself. "I'll go get some painkillers. You'll be alright, darling."

He planted a kiss on my forehead, and then he was off to get the drugs. As he walked away, once again I asked myself why it was so hard to kill him. This time, I didn't evade the question. I couldn't get myself to kill him because he was different from every other man I'd ever met. He catered to my every need, reminding me of how much my father had loved me.

I was falling in love with Anthony Esteban—the very same man I'd set out to kill.

CHAPTER SEVEN

"Wakey wakey!" Anthony said in a sing-song voice that roused me out of sleep.

The pills he'd brought me probably had sedatives in them, because I fell asleep only a few moments after I'd taken them. My eyes narrowed open, and I looked up at him. He sat in a reverse position on a stool to the right of the bed. He watched me keenly, with a cigarette oozing out smoke between his lips.

I gaped at him. He'd once told me he didn't smoke. Something didn't seem right.

"Tony?" I called.

He puffed out a thick cloud of smoke, and amidst the murk I could see his face twisting with a dark smile. "Yes, darling?"

I made to raise myself off the bed, but an iron grip around my wrists held me back in place. Simultaneously, the clang of metal met my ears, and even without looking up to confirm, I knew I'd been cuffed to the bedframe. But why?

"Sleep well, darling?" Tony asked, sarcasm dripping out of his mouth at the mention of the endearment term.

I lay still, not letting my nerviness show. "What is this about?"

Tony rose from the chair and advanced toward me. "Officer Crystal, you deserve a standing ovation, don't you?"

"What are you talking about?" I asked.

"Gregory Martinez," he said. "Rings a bell?"

I decided against answering.

"Let me remind you," he said.

"No need," I said. "I know who he was."

"No, you don't!" he retorted. "Because if you did, you'd know what his last name was. Esteban! Gregory Martinez Esteban!"

He dropped his cigarette to the floor and crushed it underneath his boot. His mood had suddenly turned a thousand shades darker. He gritted his teeth and squared his shoulders, his eyes burning a hole through me. I felt no different from how a squirrel would feel just before being ripped apart by a lion.

"Maybe you should have been more thorough with your research before setting out to kill me right after you killed my kid brother." He slammed his fist into the wall.

I cringed. "I didn't know--"

36

"Would it have made a difference?" he asked. "Let me answer that for you. No! And you know why? Because you're just some horny slut of a cop who's so obsessed with pleasure and pain that she finishes off petty criminals right after fucking them! What were you thinking? That it'd be so easy getting rid of me? You thought you could ride me off into the sunset, kill me, and then ride back off into the sunset, didn't you? Well, think again."

He huffed, raking his hands through his hair and sweeping them backward, away from his face. "My brother was not as stupid as you thought, bitch! While I was still serving my prison sentence, he wrote me a letter in detail, telling me he had his suspicion about an officer he was dating named Crystal. And guess what? You killed him the day after I received the letter. I had a feeling I would be your next kill, so all I did was wait. And I wasn't disappointed. I knew you staged the little car bump nonsense and I knew that all you wanted was to put a bullet through my chest and move on to the next."

He reached behind him and yanked out a pistol.

"Anthony," I pleaded.

"There's nothing you can say that will change this outcome. You are just as guilty as the criminals you took away. You are a murderer just like us. Maybe even worse. And now you will be one less cop to worry about," he said, aiming his pistol at me. "Just like the cop I killed back in ninety-eight right here in Nashville. Some stupid copper trying to get my gang and I when we were fleeing from a convenience store robbery. I hate cops! They're filthy liars."

My eyes widened at his confession.

He huffed out a breath. "What? Didn't think I only committed minor crimes, did you?"

But that wasn't why his confession had startled me so much. The man he'd killed was my father. Anthony was the culprit who'd been at large for twenty years already. If there was one person who needed to be killed, it was he—the man who'd killed my father. I was certain he couldn't have been referring to any other officer but my dad because my father was the only officer who was killed in Nashville that year.

"I am one guy you don't wanna fuck with," he continued. "But it's too late to sound the warning now 'cause you already did."

Bile rose in my throat as I watched him speak. I would never forgive myself for being so lenient with the wrong person. And even worse, I had his seed in my womb. My dad's grandchild was the seed of his murderer. It literally made me sick. I did everything in my power to hold back the vomit. As dreadful as the news of my pregnancy was, maybe this was just what I needed—my only way out.

I looked up at him, forcing my mind away from the fact that a gruesome killer was just about to end me. "I'm pregnant with your child, Anthony."

"I'm not falling for your tricks--"

"The test result is in the bathroom cabinet."

I watched him intently, studying his reaction to my confession. He was almost forty and without a child. Surely, he would rethink his decision to kill me. And he did. Without another word, he tucked his pistol into his waistline and stormed out of the room.

A moment alone was just what I needed. I was no stranger to handcuffs and my hands were petite enough to slide right out of them. Freeing myself, I hurried over to my ankle-length boot where I'd hidden my SIG Sauer handgun. I yanked it out and returned to lie on the bed. I held the pistol behind my head, with my hands against the cuffs. I slightly heaved my body upward, so my head concealed my unrestrained hands and the pistol. Inviting Anthony over to my house was a horrid mistake. What if he wandered into the basement and found the evidence board? Finding out I was Oliver Jameson's daughter would only make him kill me faster than he'd planned.

As these thoughts continued to whirl around my mind, I heard the sound of footsteps advancing toward the door. I shifted my body into a more natural posture, making sure to hide the gun behind my full blonde hair.

Anthony strode in, his gaze immediately darting across the room to where I lay.

He tilted his head sideways, approaching me with a wary look in his eyes. "What tha--"

He reached behind him to grab his gun, but I beat him to the first shot. My hands sprang out of hiding, aiming the gun at his chest and swiftly pulling the trigger. He dropped to the floor, blood oozing out of the bullet hole in his chest. I stared at him in his now lifeless state, and oddly, the part of me that had cared about him was gone.

He deserved a parting gift. And what better than a final crime in his name? He had been a criminal all his life, so it would only make sense that he'd died doing the things he loved, namely breaking in and a rape attempt. Dropping my gun on the white dressing table on the left side of the room, I dedicated the next five minutes to staging a perfect robbery scene. A few broken and displaced properties painted the perfect picture. Done, I picked up my cellphone from the dressing table and dialed my office. While I waited for someone to pick up the phone, I started to pace the length of the room.

"Nashville Police Department," a voice said from the receiver.

I stopped pacing. "I'm calling to report a break-in."

Out of the corner of my eyes, I saw Anthony's arm outstretching toward his gun on the floor.

"Shit!" I cursed, dropping my phone to the floor while I sprinted across the room for my gun. Fetching it, I whirled around and fired multiple shots into his chest. And once the final shot boomed around the room, I realized it hadn't come from my pistol.

A bullet had sailed through my flesh, burying itself in my chest. I whimpered, my body thudding to the ground. I knew this was it, that there was nothing left to fight for. I didn't know how much longer I would still draw breath, but I knew I would not live to fire another shot. My whole world started to fade to black, and as my eyelids fell heavily over my now glistening eyes, I let the darkness engulf me.

Thank you for your purchase! Here are some additional books by the author.

Get More Books

Guides

Unleashing Essential Oils: With Extra Invaluable Beauty Tips

E-book Supplier for First Time Home Buyer

My Diet Your Diet Our Diet

Experience of Life vs. Expert Advice

Children Book

Little Cupcake's First Day

Novels and Novellas

Partially Broken Never Destroyed I, II, III, IV, V, VI

Alyce Leaves Wonderland

Short Stories

After Dawn Breaks

www.ingramcontent.com/pod-product-compliance
Lightning Source LLC
Chambersburg PA
CBHW050917120626
46552CB00004B/1622